TO:_____

FROM:_____

# INTRODUCTION

## by Dick Van Dyke

One of the very best things about Christmastime is a touching Christmas story. I think you'll enjoy the entertaining and intriguing way that *Mr. Finnegan's Giving Chest* reminds us of the more important things in life and encourages us to reach beyond ourselves.

Also, I have always felt that a great story can only be better with great imagery. Ever since my experience of dancing with penguins in the movie *Mary Poppins*, I have been fascinated with techniques of illustration and special effects. In fact, for many years one of my favorite hobbies has been creating computer-generated imagery and 3D animation.

So, when I was given the chance to help create this children's Christmas story, I was thrilled. I realized it was an opportunity to merge my love of storytelling, computer art, and Christmas.

I hope you'll enjoy *Mr. Finnegan's Giving Chest* and remember that the Christmas spirit doesn't need to end after December 25.

*I dedicate my efforts on this book to my wife, Stephanie; my parents; my family;
and my children, Matthew and Jacob. Most of all, I dedicate this to my Father in Heaven
for helping me through to the completion of this book.*
—Dan Farr

*Thank you, Lorie, for your love and support. To my children, Ryan, Kyle, and Cameron,
I dedicate this work; may you take hold of the message in this book.*
—Chris Creek

*To my wife, my parents, and everyone else who tries to
leave the world a little better than they found it.*
—Chad Smith

Graphics Cards provided by Nvidia Corporation. www.nvidia.com
All 3D images were created with DAZ|Studio. www.dazstudio.com

Text and Illustration © 2005 DAZ Productions

Visit us at shadowmountain.com

**Library of Congress Cataloging-in-Publication Data**
Farr, Dan.
  Mr. Finnegan's giving chest / Dan Farr.
    p.  cm.
  Summary: On Christmas Eve, with help from a mysterious toymaker and a magic box, a young girl learns about the spirit of giving.
  ISBN-10  1-59038-555-1 (hardbound : alk. paper)
  ISBN-13  978-1-59038-555-5 (hardbound : alk. paper)
  [1. Christmas—Fiction. 2. Magic—Fiction. 3. Generosity—Fiction.] I. Title: Mister Finnegan's giving chest. II. Title.
  PZ7.F2398Mrf 2005
  [Fic]—dc22                                              2005025793

Printed in the United States of America
Inland Press, Menomonee Falls, WI

10     9     8     7     6     5     4     3     2

# MR. FINNEGAN'S
# GIVING CHEST

### BY DAN FARR

### MR. FINNEGAN BASED ON
# DICK VAN DYKE

SHADOW
MOUNTAIN

**N**ot again," muttered the white-haired toymaker as the worn handle fell off the wooden chest he was carrying. He struggled to balance the chest as the handle clattered to the floor. "How many times will I have to repair this old thing?" He put the chest on a cluttered table, carefully opened the lid, and removed a snow globe set in a hand-carved wooden base. Shaking it, he looked inside.

As the swirling snow settled, the small town of Pinebough appeared. The toymaker adjusted his spectacles and peered closer as the tiny town came to life under the spell of the falling snow. Three children ran down an icy street, two chasing the other. The toymaker flinched as a snowball splattered on the neck of the boy being chased. "That sure was mean," he sighed, and then looked at his companion, a mechanical dog fashioned from a patchwork of parts. "This won't be easy, Switch," the toymaker warned. "They're almost here. I'd better hurry and get this handle fixed." He set the globe down and reached for his tools.

Outside, the faint sound of bells jingled above muffled voices and Christmas carolers. This was Christmas Eve, and a magical feeling filled the air. Most people might have explained it as holiday excitement, but some knew that it was more. Much more.

**E**xactly as the toymaker's globe had shown, three children raced through the town. Maggie hurled a hard-packed snowball, which splattered squarely on Jake's neck. Shivering, he darted down an alley. Maggie followed closely as Doug lumbered behind. Suddenly, Jake found his escape blocked by a wooden fence at the end of the alley.

"Where's our money?" Maggie demanded.

Jake gasped, "I told you I don't have any!"

Maggie laughed. "Well, poor boy, how can I keep Doug from beating you up, then?"

Doug sneered and cracked his thick knuckles. But Jake quickly squeezed through a slit in the fence and bolted off before Doug could get his meaty hands on him. Maggie attempted to follow, but her bulky coat caught in the fence. Doug snickered as Maggie's face burned with anger.

"Laugh it up, chubby," she said. "And just wait till I get out!"

Doug scowled. "If you're going to call me chubby, then I won't be here when you do."

Maggie responded, "Okay, *tubby*, get me out of here!"

**W**ith that last insult, Doug turned to leave Maggie in her predicament. But something caught his eye, and he paused. "Hey, Maggie, did you notice where we are?" He pointed to a nearby building. "Just outside the haunted old Finnegan place." He looked her in the eye. "They say that sometimes you can hear noises inside, but if you sneak in . . . nothing's there."

Just then, a stack of boxes tipped over nearby, and a cat shot out from behind. Growing afraid, Maggie struggled to free herself. Eyes wide, Doug glanced once more at Maggie and took off running. He shouted back, "Maybe you'll think twice before calling me *tubby*." As his footsteps faded in the distance, Maggie began to shiver, but not from the cold. She wriggled again and then froze in fear as the door to the building creaked open.

Out rolled Switch. Maggie's heart thumped faster as the feisty assembly of mechanical parts scrambled toward her, his wheels squealing loudly. He yapped with a metallic bark that sounded like it came from inside an empty can. He looked and sounded so funny that Maggie couldn't decide whether to scream or laugh. Then a white-haired man appeared from behind the door. "Switch! Knock that off or you'll scare the little troublemaker before I do." Leaning on the open door, he looked suspiciously over his spectacles at Maggie and added, "Dogs are a great judge of character, you know."

Maggie gulped, "Are you a . . . a ghost?"

"A ghost?" The man chuckled. "Sure. The Ghost of Christmas Past. Boo!" He laughed again. "Actually, I'm a toymaker, and I secretly use this place every year to help Santa prepare for Christmas."

"I don't believe in Santa Claus," Maggie interrupted.

"Oh, you'll believe I'm a ghost, but you won't believe in Santa? That's funny." The man grinned, but Maggie grew impatient. "Stop talking and just get me out of here!"

The toymaker didn't seem to be in a hurry to help Maggie. "Maybe I'll just leave you stuck in that fence to think about your manners." Then, with a twinkle in his eye, he continued, "Better yet, I'll help you out—if you promise to help me in return." Maggie reluctantly agreed. Without moving from the doorway, the man asked, "Have you considered just slipping out of your jacket?"

Maggie easily slid out of her coat, wondering, *Why didn't I think of that?* As she stepped forward, Switch growled. "Switch?" she said. "That's a silly name for a . . . whatever that thing is."

The man smiled. "I made him to remind me of Pete, a little dog I once had. I put Switch together from some of the spare parts I keep around here. He was just a funny little toy until I flipped this switch on his stomach, and, well, he sort of came to life. So there you have it: Switch."

Maggie shrugged. "So what do you need me to do, anyway?"

The toymaker replied mysteriously, "Let me get something for you from the shop."

Maggie considered running off, but her curiosity overcame her, and she tried to peek inside.

"Have a look," the man called over his shoulder.

Maggie sneered, "But I might see what Santa's bringing me."

"Don't worry, there's no coal in here." He chuckled.

Maggie slowly approached the doorway. As she entered the shop, a magical, wondrous world appeared.

**M**aggie stared as if in a dream. Handcrafted toys, delicious-looking candy, and every sort of Christmas novelty filled the room from floor to ceiling. Shelves laden with mysterious trinkets sagged under the weight of their loads. Knickknacks and furnishings of all sizes, from the tiniest candy cane to a large quilt embroidered with a Christmas tree, cheerfully adorned the packed shop. More wonderful yet, many of the toys and decorations were moving, not with the typical toy-like actions Maggie was used to, but as if they were alive.

In this enchanted place, which seemed to embody all of Christmas in a single room, Switch seemed almost normal.

The man grinned proudly as Maggie stood just inside the doorway, still gazing in awe. "My name is Mr. Finnegan, and, as you can see, I make toys." He smiled warmly. "Everything you see here has a special purpose, meant just for that person who is to receive it. The trick is to match up the item to the person. And that, young lady, is done through the magic of Christmas."

There's nothing magic about Christmas. If there was, why didn't I get what I wanted last year? I was good, really good, and all Santa brought me was toys."

Mr. Finnegan replied, "Do you think Santa's the only one who can give us the gifts we want? There are some things he can't give. Santa's presents simply remind us of a much greater gift, a gift inside ourselves." Mr. Finnegan lifted the fragile wooden chest by its recently repaired handle and placed it in a wagon.

"What's *that* old thing?" Maggie asked sourly.

"This old thing is the Giving Chest. It once carried precious gifts to a newborn king. I need you to deliver it to someone."

Maggie brightened. "Is there a treasure inside?"

Mr. Finnegan raised a brow. "For some people, indeed there is."

As he turned to write down the delivery address, Maggie quickly peeked inside the chest. It was empty. She looked around the shop. "Don't you have anything better for me to deliver?"

"Nothing better," Mr. Finnegan replied. "Because of its noble heritage, this chest can magically deliver gifts for people in need. Here's the address. Hurry before it's too late."

"So if it's magic, can I get a gift from it?" Maggie tried to look innocent.

Mr. Finnegan chuckled. "No, but I can get a gift for you." He went on, "You don't use the Giving Chest to get gifts for yourself; you use it to help others." Lifting the lid, he gazed inside. "Well, would you look at that!"

"What is it?" cried Maggie.

"Y ou tell me," Mr. Finnegan replied, opening the chest wider to reveal a beautiful, gold-chained pendant with a heart-shaped diamond. He gestured for Maggie to pick it up. As she did, she realized it was identical to the necklace her grandmother had always worn. She remembered her grandmother's dying wish that her pendant be used to help someone in need. But, even though the pendant was very valuable, Maggie's father had wanted it buried with her grandmother, and so it was.

Maggie glared. "This was my grandmother's. How did you get it?"

"I didn't," Mr. Finnegan explained. "You saw for yourself, it came from the chest. I imagine she wants you to have it."

"My grandma's gone. She died last Christmas," Maggie argued. "Are you saying a ghost gave me this?"

"No, not a ghost," he replied. "More like an angel. And she isn't gone, just gone on ahead."

Maggie's eyes narrowed. "You're playing tricks on me. How come you know so much, anyway?"

Mr. Finnegan smiled. "You don't get to my stage in life without knowing something about death, Maggie."

"I never told you my name." Maggie's eyes filled with angry tears. "I don't believe in angels. I hate Christmas, and I hate you!" She spun around, turning her back on the old man. "Our deal's off! I don't believe in any of this."

Mr. Finnegan followed as she stomped out the front door. "Just because you don't believe in something doesn't mean it's not real," he whispered. Then, leaving the wagon and chest outside, he disappeared back into his shop.

Maggie looked back. Did that chest really have magical powers, or did Mr. Finnegan just slip the pendant inside without her seeing? Was this really her grandmother's pendant? If so, how did the old man get it? Maggie knew that to find the answers to those questions, she needed to make the delivery. Sighing, she put the pendant into her pocket and went back to get the wagon.

O n Maggie's way to the address, she saw a woman shivering on a step. Just for an instant, Maggie's eyes met hers; then Maggie lowered her gaze. But the image of the woman's deep-blue eyes still burned in her mind. They looked familiar somehow. As Maggie passed, the woman asked if she had any money to spare.

"No," Maggie responded.

The woman looked at the chest. "But I'm so cold."

"I don't have anything for you," Maggie rudely replied, opening the chest to prove it. But to Maggie's surprise, inside lay the Christmas tree quilt she had seen earlier in the shop.

In shock, Maggie handed the soft quilt to the woman. She wrapped it around herself and smiled pleasantly at Maggie. "You're an angel. It can be hard to give away something special to someone who needs it more than you do. Thank you, my dear."

Maggie smiled slightly as she walked away. She remembered her grandmother's blue eyes and turned for another look, but the woman was gone.

Now more curious than ever, Maggie decided to test the chest on others along her way. She gave a football to a boy, a violin to a young woman, and a cane to a man with a limp. Each time Maggie opened the chest, she found a new gift, something she had seen in the toy shop. And as she gave, Maggie grew increasingly excited and happy. Something was still missing, though. This was almost too easy. Still, Maggie felt happier than she had in a long, long time.

hen Maggie saw a couple pleading with a police officer. "How can you do this to us?" the man asked. "My wife will have her baby any day now."

The officer sighed. "I'm sorry, but I'm just doing my job. Since your landlord died, his nephew says you can't stay here. He's the next of kin, and I have to do what he says."

Maggie hoped she could help, but she knew these people needed more than just a toy or trinket. In the chest she saw a large, brown envelope. She handed it to the woman, who gave her a puzzled look. Maggie shrugged. The woman opened the envelope, revealing the deed to the house and the landlord's will, which the nephew said had been lost. The landlord had left the house to the couple in gratitude for their many years of caring for him. Maggie blushed as the woman tearfully thanked her, and then she continued happily down the street.

*It's just like Mr. Finnegan said,* Maggie thought. *This chest really does give just what people need!* And with that, Maggie remembered her own gift from the chest. Excitedly, she pulled the pendant from her pocket and looked at it again. As she put it around her neck, Maggie felt warmth flow throughout her body. She smiled, knowing that her grandmother was still looking after her somehow. This pendant really was the best gift Maggie could have hoped for, after all. She decided right then that she never wanted to lose this feeling.

ack in the shop, Mr. Finnegan said to Switch, "Let's see how our girl is doing." He shook the snow globe again, and as the snow settled, he saw Maggie reach the appointed address. "I knew we could count on her," he said.

Indeed, as the globe had shown, Maggie cheerfully arrived in front of a tall doorway. She paused, thinking, *If I deliver the chest now, I'll only give to one more person. But I can help more people if I bring it back later, and nobody will know the difference.* Deep down, Maggie knew her decision was more selfish than she was admitting. She didn't want to lose the good feeling she had felt all afternoon. Mr. Finnegan would understand. Wouldn't he? She turned away from the large gray building.

Suddenly, she heard a familiar voice. It was Doug. "Escaped from the fence, huh? What's that in the wagon?" Maggie was surprised to find that in spite of how mean Doug could be sometimes, she really wanted to share with him everything he'd missed, especially the magic Giving Chest. As she boasted of the day's events, Maggie couldn't hide her excitement. She explained how the chest knew just the right gift to give when opened.

To Maggie's surprise, Doug didn't believe a word. Taunting, he snatched the chest from the wagon. "Give it back!" Maggie shrieked, grabbing at the other end. They tugged and fought until finally the fragile chest cracked and burst into pieces. Maggie stared in disbelief. She clenched her fist to give Doug the thrashing he deserved. But instead of anger, a wave of sadness overcame her as she looked at the shattered chest. Choking back tears, she said, "Just get out of here, Doug."

Doug laughed nervously. "Okay," he said, "you can keep your stupid box."

As Doug disappeared around the corner, Maggie loaded the splintered wood into the wagon. Never before had she felt so sad. Her mind began to race. Why did Doug have to spoil everything? And why didn't he believe her? Why did that old woman make her open the chest in the first place? If not for her, Maggie would have taken it straight to the address. Why had Mr. Finnegan given the chest to her, anyway? She felt herself sink even lower as she began to worry about the person who really needed the chest but wouldn't get it now because of her selfishness.

Maggie trudged back to the gray building, where a young boy answered her knock on the door. It was Jake. Seeing Maggie, he gasped, "How did you find me?"

Maggie pulled the wagon closer as Jake backed up. "Relax, I'm not here for you. I'm just delivering a chest."

Jake skeptically eyed the broken pieces of wood.

Maggie added, "I didn't even know this was your house."

"Really?" Jake asked.

Maggie looked down. "Really. And I'm sorry for being so mean."

"Want to come in?" Jake said.

So Maggie did. The house was warm and bright.

ust then a woman entered the room. "May I help you?"

Maggie explained what had happened and apologized for the broken chest. Ashamed, she tried to change the subject. "Well, you sure have a nice, big house here," she blurted out.

The woman smiled and said it was a home for orphans and homeless children. For the first time that evening, everything made sense. Now Maggie knew why Jake dressed the way he did and why Mr. Finnegan wanted her to deliver the chest here. These children must have needed a special gift. But with the chest destroyed, Maggie had failed in her mission.

Then Maggie had a thought. Her grandmother had wished her pendant could help someone. Maybe she could give it to the orphanage. But the pendant was the one thing Maggie would ever get from the broken chest. Her own grandmother had sent it to her. How could she give it away? Then Maggie remembered what the old woman had said: *It can be hard to give away something special to someone who needs it more.* She took a deep breath and handed the pendant to the woman. "This is from my grandmother."

The woman hesitated. "Are you sure? This is a very expensive necklace."

But Maggie insisted, "She would have wanted . . . I mean, she wants you to have it."

The woman smiled gratefully. "You don't know how much this means to us. Your gift will help make this Christmas a special one for the children. Thank you."

Maggie felt a new kind of joy. This was the first time she had offered something truly of herself, not from the chest. It felt different. Better. Maggie realized she had received more from the Giving Chest than just the pendant after all. She had even made a few friends along the way. Maggie smiled at Jake.

At that moment a little gray-haired dog ran into the room and looked up at Maggie, wagging his tail. The woman raised an eyebrow. "Hmm. Pete here usually doesn't pay much attention to strangers." With a twinkle in her eye, she added, "Of course, dogs are a great judge of character."

The woman became serious again. "I forgot to ask who sent the chest." Maggie told her it was a gift from Mr. Finnegan. *"Mr. Finnegan?"* The woman looked at her intently and invited Maggie to follow her to a nearby portrait on the wall. "This is a picture of my husband. Is this who sent you with the chest?" It was Mr. Finnegan.

"Yeah, that's him," Maggie said. "But if he's your husband, why didn't he just bring the chest himself?"

The woman pointed to an inscription on the frame. Maggie's eyes widened as she read it: "In memory of Nicholas Finnegan, whose service and generosity made the Finnegan Memorial Orphanage possible. Not gone, just gone on ahead. Forever our guardian."

Jake spoke up: "Maggie, you look like you just saw a ghost."

Maggie thought for a moment and then smiled. "Not a ghost. More like an angel."

aggie looked again at Mr. Finnegan's portrait and whispered, "I'm sorry for being so selfish. I don't hate you, and I don't hate Christmas. Thanks for helping me understand." And though she wasn't sure, Maggie thought she saw Mr. Finnegan wink at her. She felt a wonderful warmth come over her as if Mr. Finnegan himself were giving her a hug of approval. *This is the best feeling of all,* she thought.

As the sun set on Pinebough, the faint sound of jingling bells could be heard and that magical feeling still filled the air—the feeling that was more than just holiday excitement. But now, a few more people knew why. Mr. Finnegan shook the snow globe once again. Gazing inside, he saw the beginning of a bright, new day, where two young friends were laughing and playing. He breathed a sigh of contentment and placed the snow globe back on the shelf.

THE END

# ACKNOWLEDGMENTS

The reason this book was completed is because I am surrounded by people much more talented than I am who contributed in so many ways. I cannot name them all, but I will try to name a few. I wish to thank first and foremost Dick Van Dyke for his friendship and amazing talent, and for lending his support and ideas to this labor of love.

I value my many years of working with my business partner Chris Creek and express my thanks for his creative artwork and commitment to this project. Without Chris this book would not have been done. I will always be grateful for the long hours of poring over the story with Chad Smith, for his attention to detail and excitement for this work.

I appreciate the talented crew of DAZ Productions. I'm blessed to be a part of such a dedicated staff. Thanks to Tony Bradt, Allen Renfeldt, Rob Whisenant, Eric Allen, Greg White, Jared Buchanan, Josh Darling, Jacob Speirs, and Daniel Vest for their involvement with modeling, UV layout, texture mapping, character rigging, and scene creation. I'm also indebted to many others at DAZ who have given valuable feedback and insight to this book.

Special thanks go to Micah Henrie for his skilled scene lighting.

Thank you to Kurt Dowdle for design work, additional editing, insights, enthusiasm, and valuable connections. Thanks to Brian Harvey for his emotional support and excitement. Thanks to our 3D art community for providing additional 3D content and for making this book possible by supporting DAZ Productions. I also appreciate suggestions for the book from family, friends, and neighbors.

Thank you Shadow Mountain Publishing for seeing the value of this story and getting behind it, especially Chris Schoebinger, Richard Erickson, Sheryl Smith, Jack Lyon, and Tonya Facemyer for seeing the book through to completion and for your incredible talents.

—Dan Farr

Story by Dan Farr

3D imagery by DAZ Productions

Art direction, character design, and character modeling by Chris Creek

3D image art lead, story development, and editing by Chad Smith

All 3D images were created with DAZ|Studio: www.dazstudio.com

THE TRUE MAGIC of *The Giving Chest* can be found inside each one of us. We can reach out to others. And in doing so, we'll find that the happiness that comes from helping others is proportionate to the sacrifice we are willing to make.

If you would like to experience this magic yourself, then start your very own GIVING CHEST tradition. Find a "chest" that you and your family can use to collect money or other valuables you can use to help others in need. You can also write down ideas of things you would like to do and put them in the chest as reminders for when you are able to do them. And remember that not all gifts are financial. Your time, love, and service are often the most needed gifts.

For more information, ideas, and stories relating to *Mr. Finnegan's Giving Chest*, visit www.givingchest.com